Dear Parent:

Congratulations! Your child is taking the first steps on an exciting journey. The destination? Independent reading!

STEP INTO READING® will help your child get there. The program offers books at five levels that accompany children from their first attempts at reading to reading success. Each step includes fun stories, fiction and nonfiction, and colorful art. There are also Step into Reading Sticker Books, Step into Reading Math Readers, Step into Reading Write-In Readers, Step into Reading Phonics Readers, and Step into Reading Phonics First Steps! Boxed Sets—a complete literacy program with something to interest every child.

Learning to Read, Step by Step!

Ready to Read Preschool–Kindergarten
• big type and easy words • rhyme and rhythm • picture clues
For children who know the alphabet and are eager to begin reading.

Reading with Help Preschool–Grade 1
• basic vocabulary • short sentences • simple stories
For children who recognize familiar words and sound out new words with help.

Reading on Your Own Grades 1–3
• engaging characters • easy-to-follow plots • popular topics
For children who are ready to read on their own.

Reading Paragraphs Grades 2–3
• challenging vocabulary • short paragraphs • exciting stories
For newly independent readers who read simple sentences with confidence.

Ready for Chapters Grades 2–4
• chapters • longer paragraphs • full-color art
For children who want to take the plunge into chapter books but still like colorful pictures.

STEP INTO READING® is designed to give every child a successful reading experience. The grade levels are only guides. Children can progress through the steps at their own speed, developing confidence in their reading, no matter what their grade.

Remember, a lifetime love of reading starts with a single step!

For Frankie, Kevin Ryan, and Ava
—M.L.

www.randomhouse.com/kids/disney

www.stepintoreading.com

Educators and librarians, for a variety of teaching tools, visit us at
www.randomhouse.com/teachers

Library of Congress Cataloging-in-Publication Data

Lagonegro, Melissa.
Just keep swimming / by Melissa Lagonegro.
    p. cm. — (Step into reading. Step 1)
Summary: When Nemo worries that his too-small fin will keep him off the school swim team, his friend Dory encourages him.
ISBN 0-7364-2319-2—ISBN 0-7364-8041-2 (lib. bdg.)
[1. Fishes—Fiction. 2. Swimming—Fiction. 3. Friendship—Fiction. 4. Stories in rhyme.]
I. Title. II. Series.
PZ8.3.L214Ju 2005   [E]—dc22   2004008588

Printed in the United States of America 27 26 25 24

STEP INTO READING, RANDOM HOUSE, and the Random House colophon are registered trademarks of Random House, Inc.

Just Keep Swimming

XZ
IR
L

by Melissa Lagonegro
illustrated by Atelier Philippe Harchy

Random House 🏠 New York

Nemo has a dream.
He wants to join
the school swim team.

But Nemo has
a little fin.

He thinks that
he will never win.

Dory helps Nemo.

She teaches him
to go, go, go!

Nemo races and races.

Nemo chases and chases.

"Just keep swimming,"
Dory sings.

But Nemo thinks
of other things.

"I will never win.

I have a bad fin."

"Just keep swimming!"
Dory cries.

So Nemo tries . . .

and tries . . .

. . . and tries.

Nemo races and races.

Nemo chases and chases.

Yippee! Yahoo!

His dream comes true.

Nemo makes the team.

Can Nemo win the
first-place prize?

"Just keep swimming!"
Dory cries.

Watch him race.

Watch him chase.

Watch as Nemo wins
first place!